W9-AUJ-912

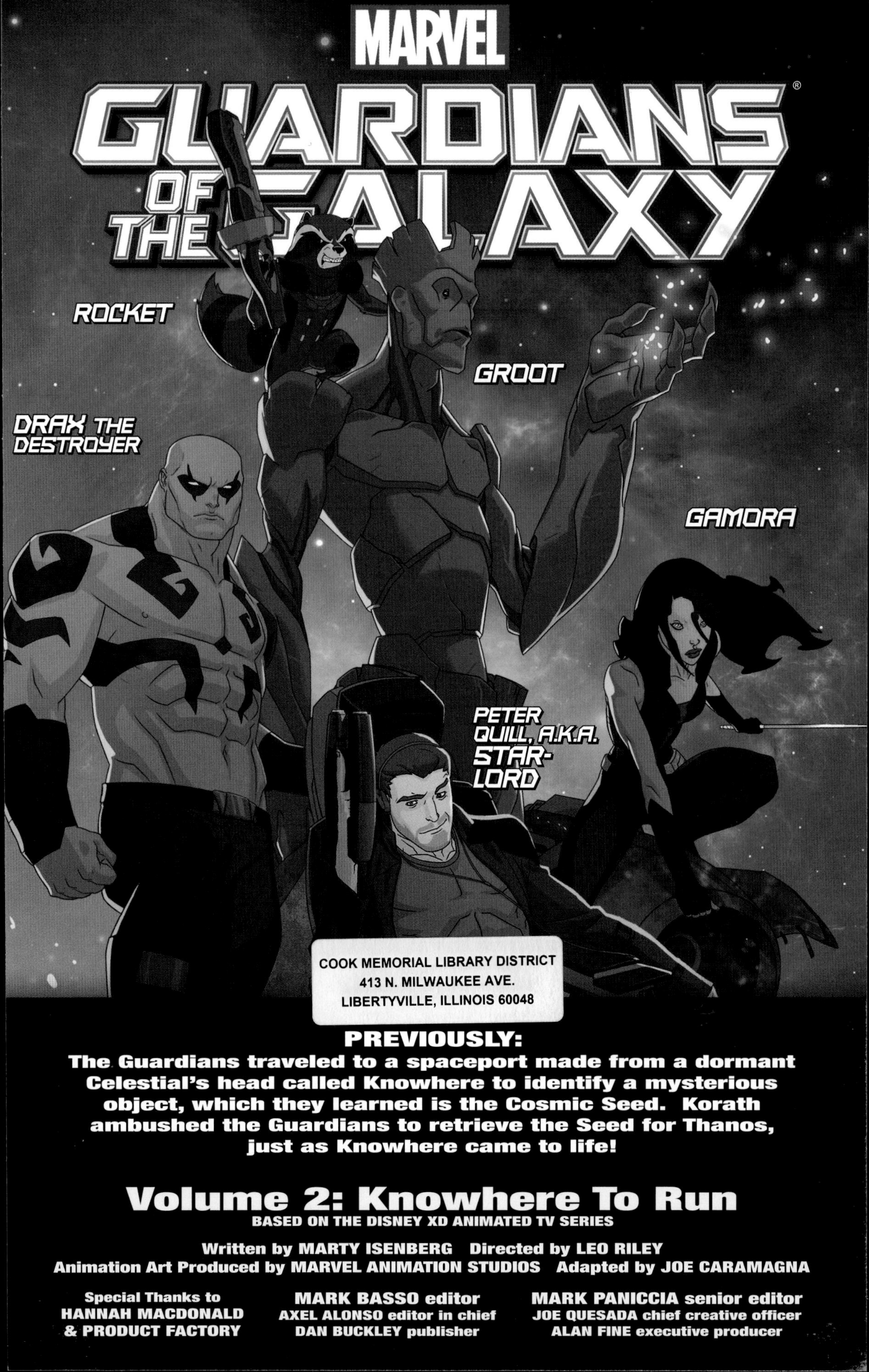
MARVEL
GUARDIANS OF THE GALAXY
ROCKET
GROOT
DRAX THE DESTROYER
GAMORA
PETER QUILL, A.K.A. STAR-LORD

PREVIOUSLY:

The Guardians traveled to a spaceport made from a dormant Celestial's head called Knowhere to identify a mysterious object, which they learned is the Cosmic Seed. Korath ambushed the Guardians to retrieve the Seed for Thanos, just as Knowhere came to life!

Volume 2: Knowhere To Run

BASED ON THE DISNEY XD ANIMATED TV SERIES

Written by MARTY ISENBERG Directed by LEO RILEY
Animation Art Produced by MARVEL ANIMATION STUDIOS Adapted by JOE CARAMAGNA

Special Thanks to HANNAH MACDONALD & PRODUCT FACTORY
MARK BASSO editor
AXEL ALONSO editor in chief
DAN BUCKLEY publisher
MARK PANICCIA senior editor
JOE QUESADA chief creative officer
ALAN FINE executive producer

ABDOPUBLISHING.COM

Reinforced library bound edition published in 2018 by Spotlight,
a division of ABDO, PO Box 398166, Minneapolis, Minnesota 55439.
Spotlight produces high-quality reinforced library bound editions for
schools and libraries. Published by agreement with Marvel Characters, Inc.

Printed in the United States of America, North Mankato, Minnesota.
042017
092017

marvelkids.com
© 2017 MARVEL

PUBLISHER'S CATALOGING IN PUBLICATION DATA

Names: Isenberg, Marty ; Caramagna, Joe, authors. | Marvel Animation, illustrator.
Title: Knowhere to Run / writers: Marty Isenberg ; Joe Caramagna ; art: Marvel
    Animation.
Description: Reinforced library bound edition. | Minneapolis, Minnesota : Spotlight,
    2018. | Series: Guardians of the galaxy ; volume 2
Summary: After the Cosmic Seed caused Knowhere to be awakened and Groot to
    be overpowered by its energies, Korath kidnaps Star-Lord and Gamora, and
    Cosmo uses Knowhere technology to help Drax, Rocket, and Groot on a rescue
    mission.
Identifiers: LCCN 2017931207 | ISBN 9781532140716 (lib. bdg.)
Subjects: LCSH: Superheroes--Juvenile fiction. | Adventure and adventurers--
    Juvenile fiction. | Comic books, strips, etc.--Juvenile fiction. | Graphic novels--
    Juvenile fiction.
Classification: DDC 741.5--dc23
LC record available at https://lccn.loc.gov/2017931207

Spotlight

A Division of ABDO
abdopublishing.com

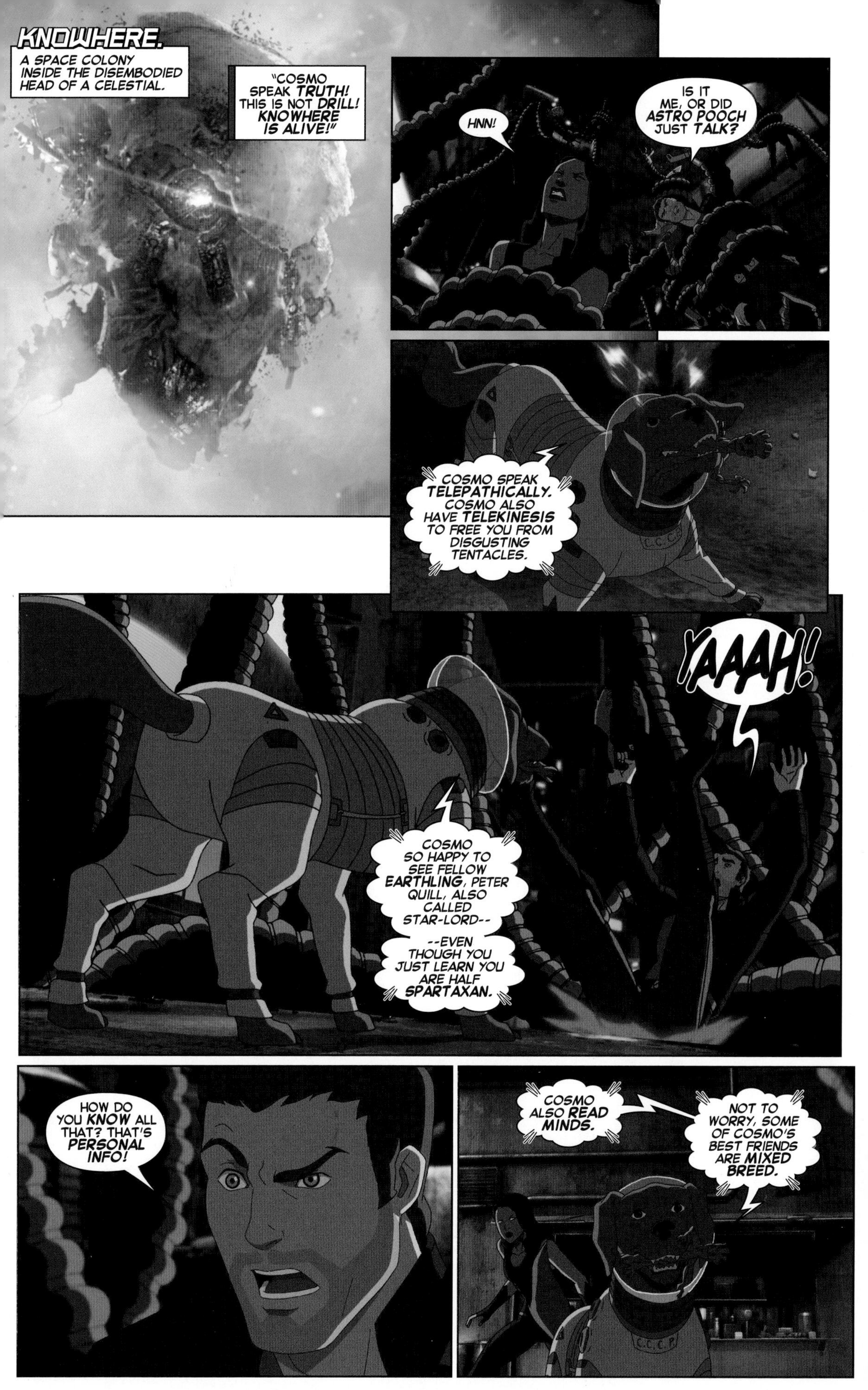
KNOWHERE.
A SPACE COLONY INSIDE THE DISEMBODIED HEAD OF A CELESTIAL.
"COSMO SPEAK TRUTH! THIS IS NOT DRILL! KNOWHERE IS ALIVE!"
HNN!
IS IT ME, OR DID ASTRO POOCH JUST TALK?
COSMO SPEAK TELEPATHICALLY. COSMO ALSO HAVE TELEKINESIS TO FREE YOU FROM DISGUSTING TENTACLES.
YAAAH!
COSMO SO HAPPY TO SEE FELLOW EARTHLING, PETER QUILL, ALSO CALLED STAR-LORD--
--EVEN THOUGH YOU JUST LEARN YOU ARE HALF SPARTAXAN.
HOW DO YOU KNOW ALL THAT? THAT'S PERSONAL INFO!
COSMO ALSO READ MINDS.
NOT TO WORRY, SOME OF COSMO'S BEST FRIENDS ARE MIXED BREED.

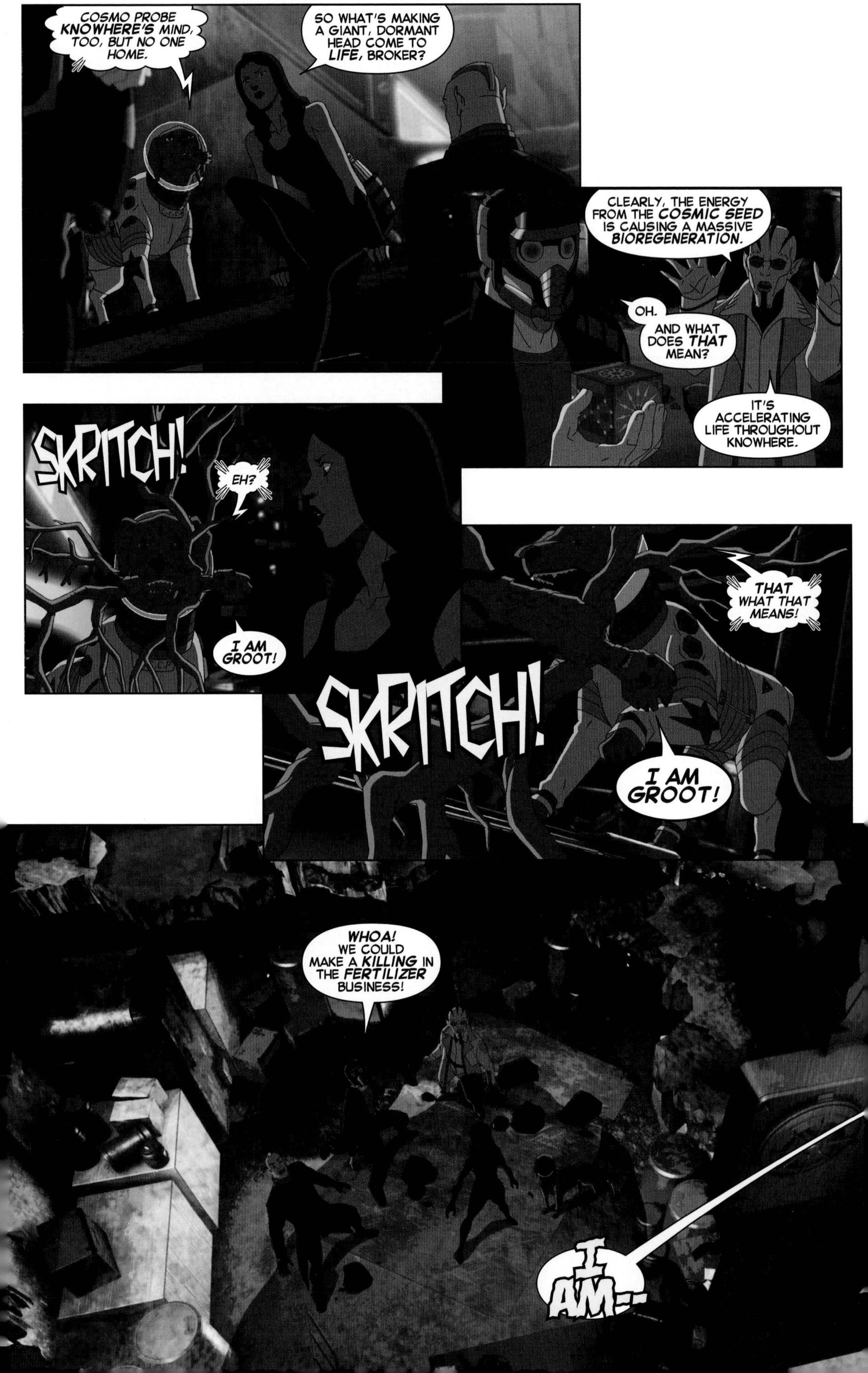
COSMO PROBE KNOWHERE'S MIND, TOO, BUT NO ONE HOME.
SO WHAT'S MAKING A GIANT, DORMANT HEAD COME TO LIFE, BROKER?
CLEARLY, THE ENERGY FROM THE COSMIC SEED IS CAUSING A MASSIVE BIOREGENERATION.
OH.
AND WHAT DOES THAT MEAN?
IT'S ACCELERATING LIFE THROUGHOUT KNOWHERE.
SKRITCH!
EH?
I AM GROOT!
THAT WHAT THAT MEANS!
SKRITCH!
I AM GROOT!
WHOA! WE COULD MAKE A KILLING IN THE FERTILIZER BUSINESS!
I AM--

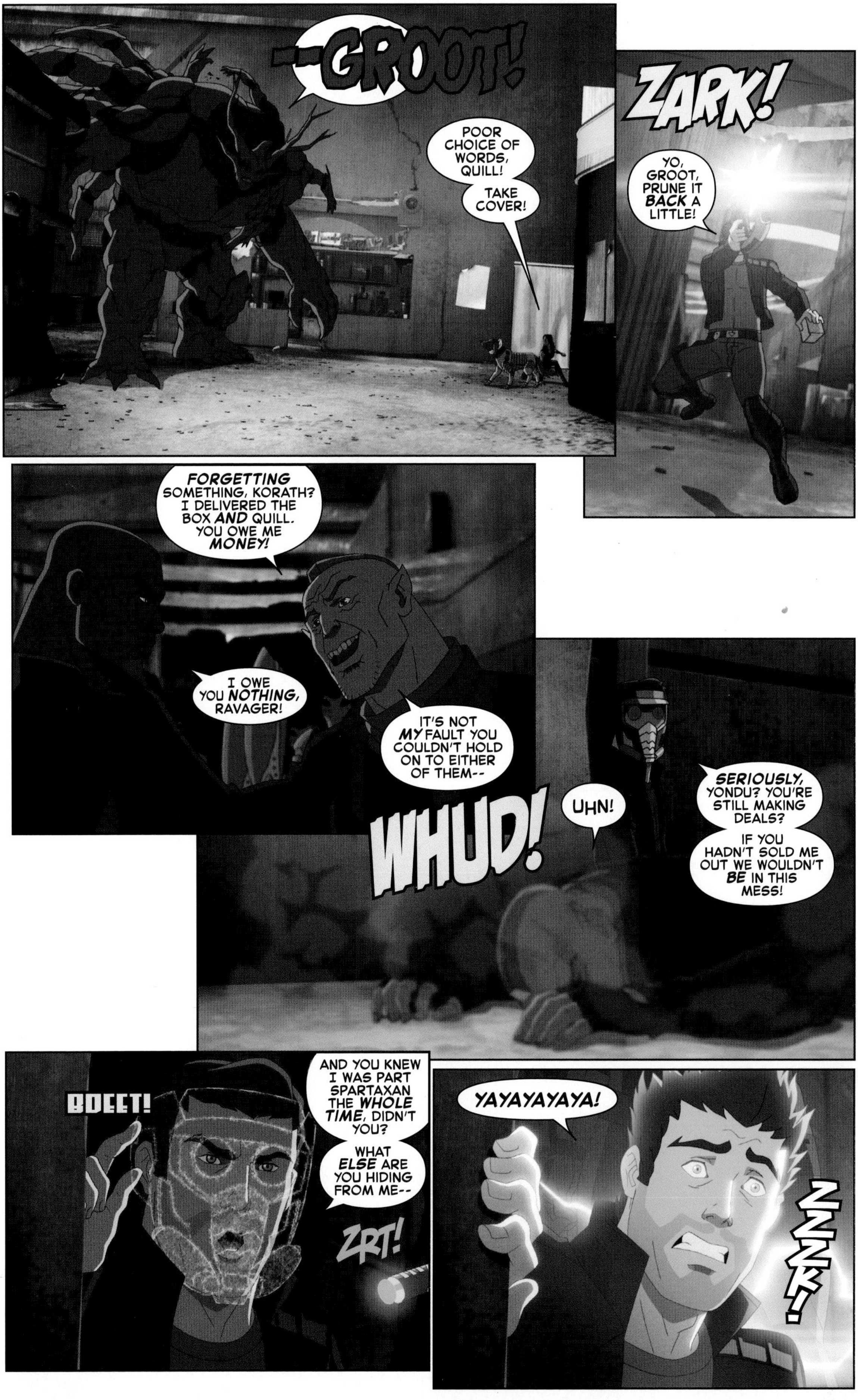
--GROOT!
POOR CHOICE OF WORDS, QUILL!
TAKE COVER!
ZARK!
YO, GROOT, PRUNE IT BACK A LITTLE!
FORGETTING SOMETHING, KORATH? I DELIVERED THE BOX AND QUILL. YOU OWE ME MONEY!
I OWE YOU NOTHING, RAVAGER!
IT'S NOT MY FAULT YOU COULDN'T HOLD ON TO EITHER OF THEM--
WHUD!
UHN!
SERIOUSLY, YONDU? YOU'RE STILL MAKING DEALS?
IF YOU HADN'T SOLD ME OUT WE WOULDN'T BE IN THIS MESS!
BDEET!
AND YOU KNEW I WAS PART SPARTAXAN THE WHOLE TIME, DIDN'T YOU?
WHAT ELSE ARE YOU HIDING FROM ME--
ZRT!
YAYAYAYAYA!
ZZZZK!

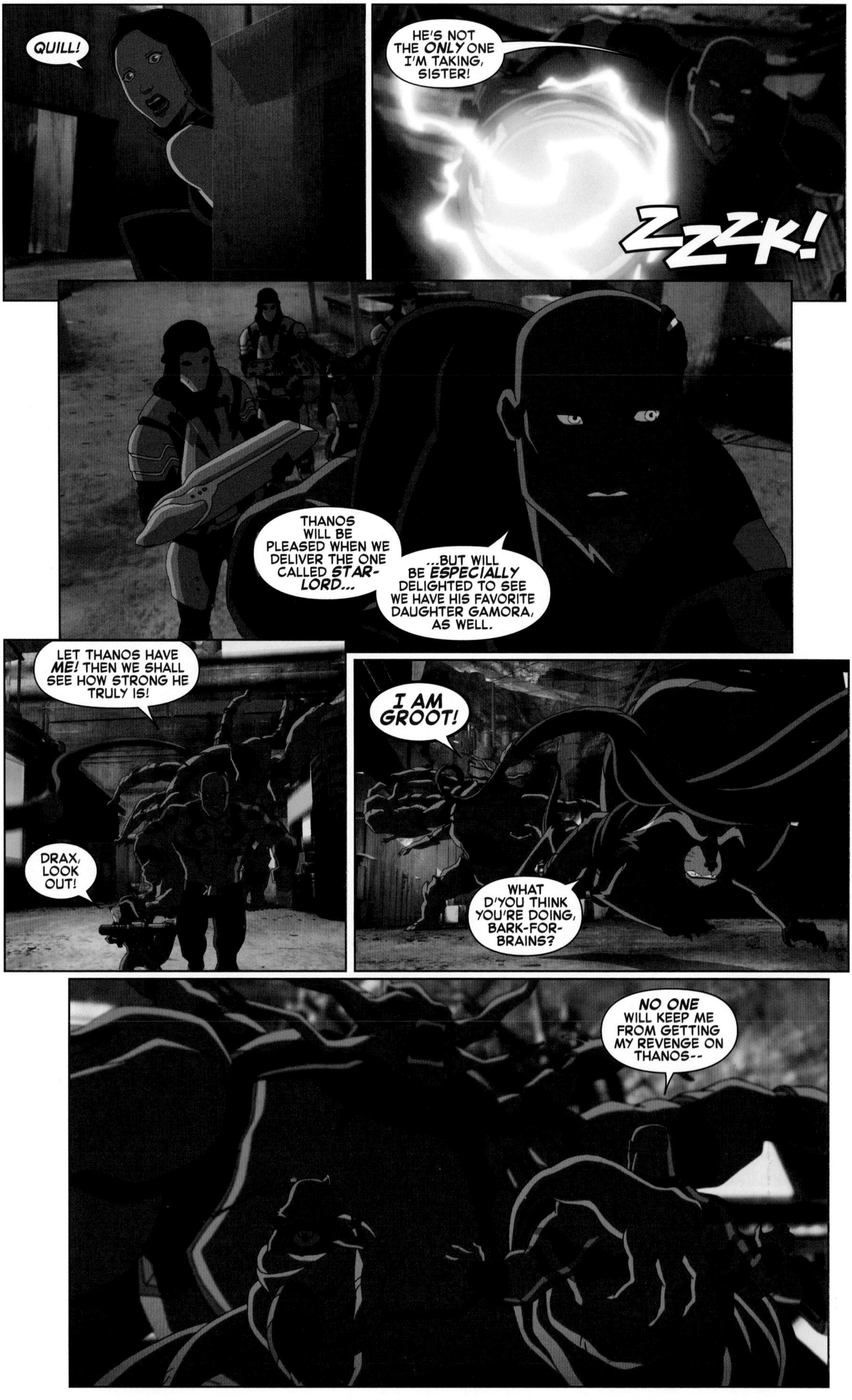
QUILL!
HE'S NOT THE ONLY ONE I'M TAKING, SISTER!
ZZZK!
THANOS WILL BE PLEASED WHEN WE DELIVER THE ONE CALLED STAR-LORD...
...BUT WILL BE ESPECIALLY DELIGHTED TO SEE WE HAVE HIS FAVORITE DAUGHTER GAMORA, AS WELL.
LET THANOS HAVE ME! THEN WE SHALL SEE HOW STRONG HE TRULY IS!
DRAX, LOOK OUT!
I AM GROOT!
WHAT D'YOU THINK YOU'RE DOING, BARK-FOR-BRAINS?
NO ONE WILL KEEP ME FROM GETTING MY REVENGE ON THANOS--

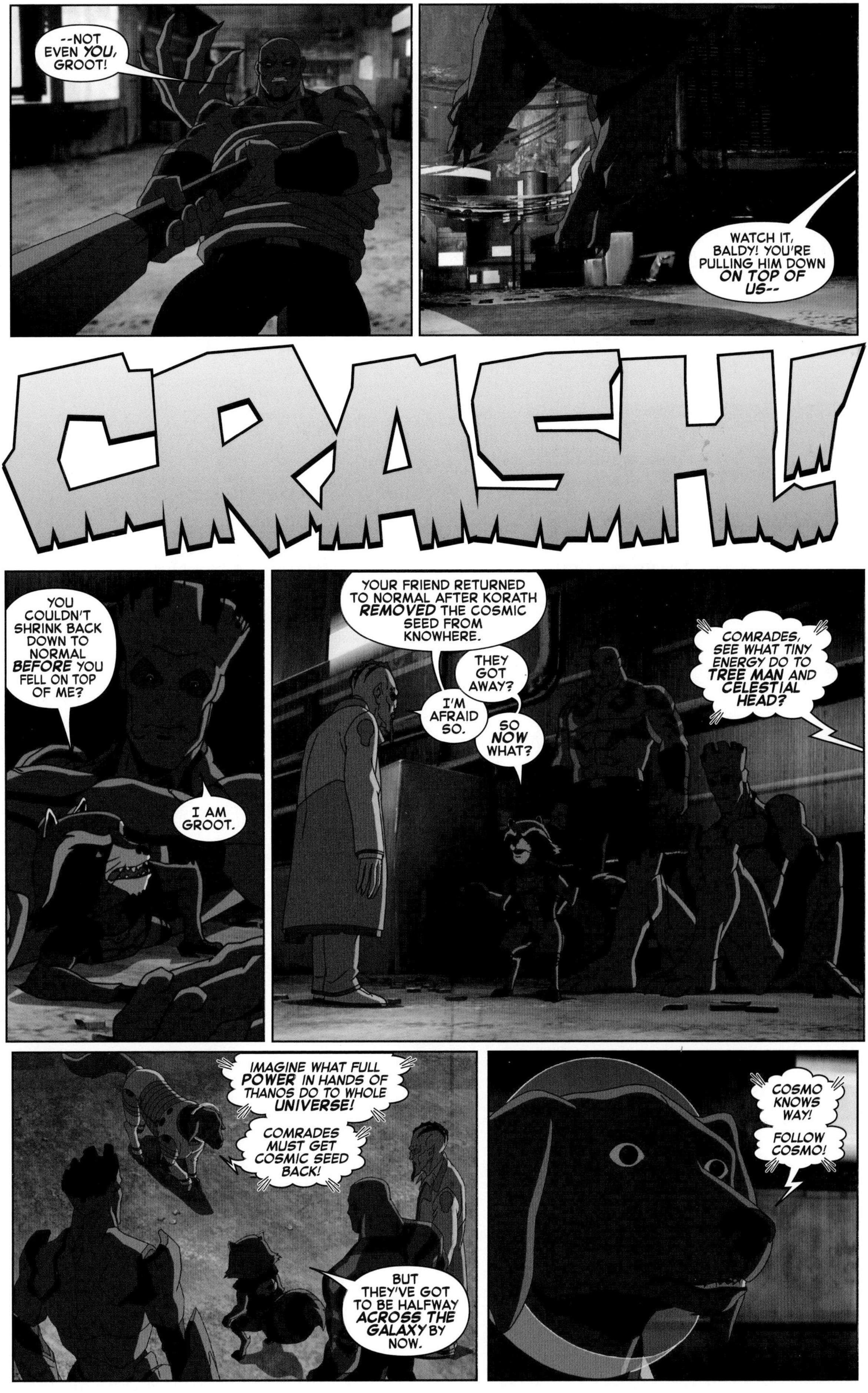
--NOT EVEN YOU, GROOT!
WATCH IT, BALDY! YOU'RE PULLING HIM DOWN ON TOP OF US--
CRASH!
YOU COULDN'T SHRINK BACK DOWN TO NORMAL BEFORE YOU FELL ON TOP OF ME?
I AM GROOT.
YOUR FRIEND RETURNED TO NORMAL AFTER KORATH REMOVED THE COSMIC SEED FROM KNOWHERE.
THEY GOT AWAY?
I'M AFRAID SO.
SO NOW WHAT?
COMRADES, SEE WHAT TINY ENERGY DO TO TREE MAN AND CELESTIAL HEAD?
IMAGINE WHAT FULL POWER IN HANDS OF THANOS DO TO WHOLE UNIVERSE!
COMRADES MUST GET COSMIC SEED BACK!
BUT THEY'VE GOT TO BE HALFWAY ACROSS THE GALAXY BY NOW.
COSMO KNOWS WAY!
FOLLOW COSMO!

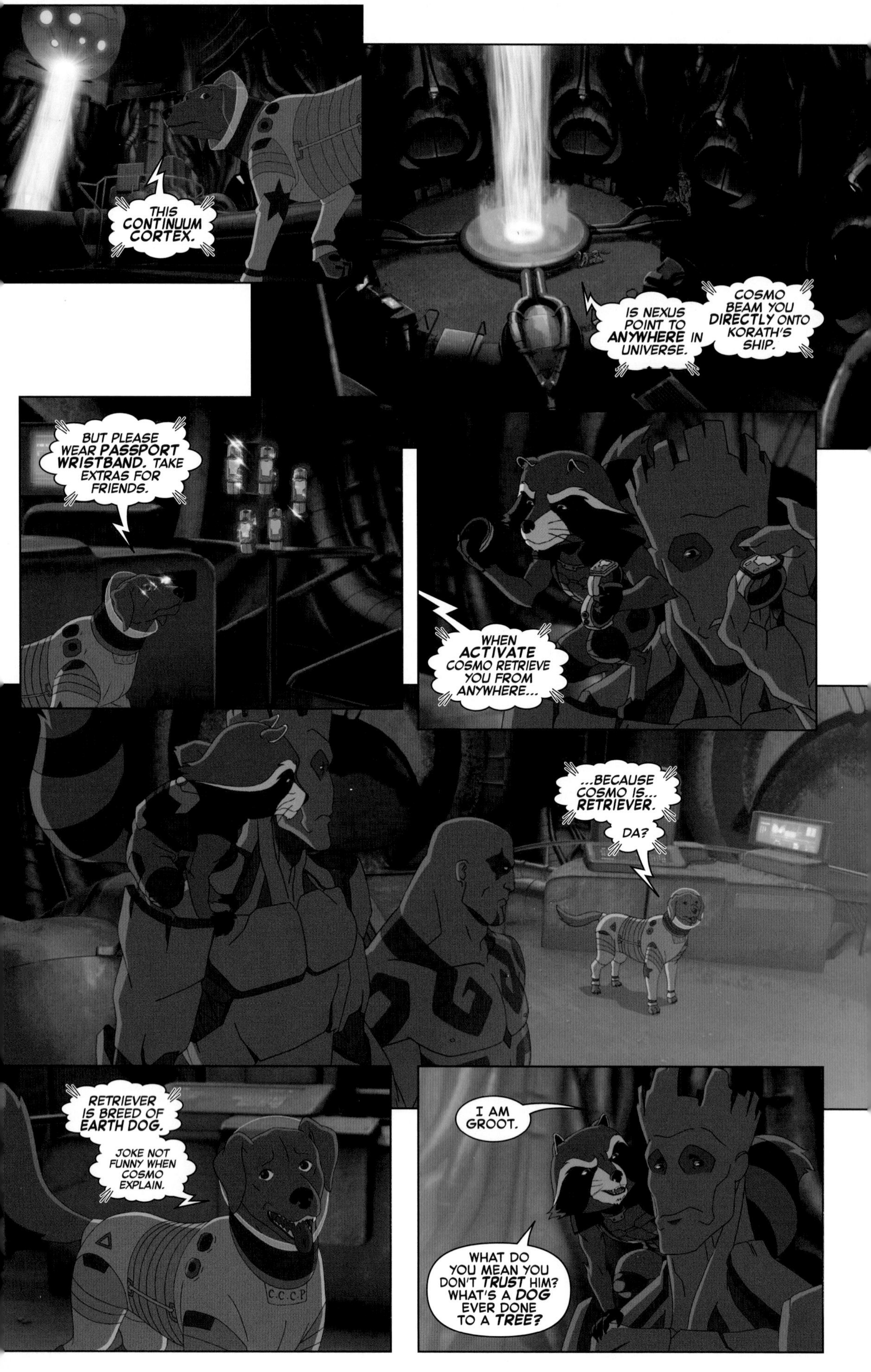
THIS CONTINUUM CORTEX.
IS NEXUS POINT TO ANYWHERE IN UNIVERSE.
COSMO BEAM YOU DIRECTLY ONTO KORATH'S SHIP.
BUT PLEASE WEAR PASSPORT WRISTBAND. TAKE EXTRAS FOR FRIENDS.
WHEN ACTIVATE COSMO RETRIEVE YOU FROM ANYWHERE...
...BECAUSE COSMO IS... RETRIEVER.
DA?
RETRIEVER IS BREED OF EARTH DOG.
JOKE NOT FUNNY WHEN COSMO EXPLAIN.
C.C.C.P.
I AM GROOT.
WHAT DO YOU MEAN YOU DON'T TRUST HIM? WHAT'S A DOG EVER DONE TO A TREE?

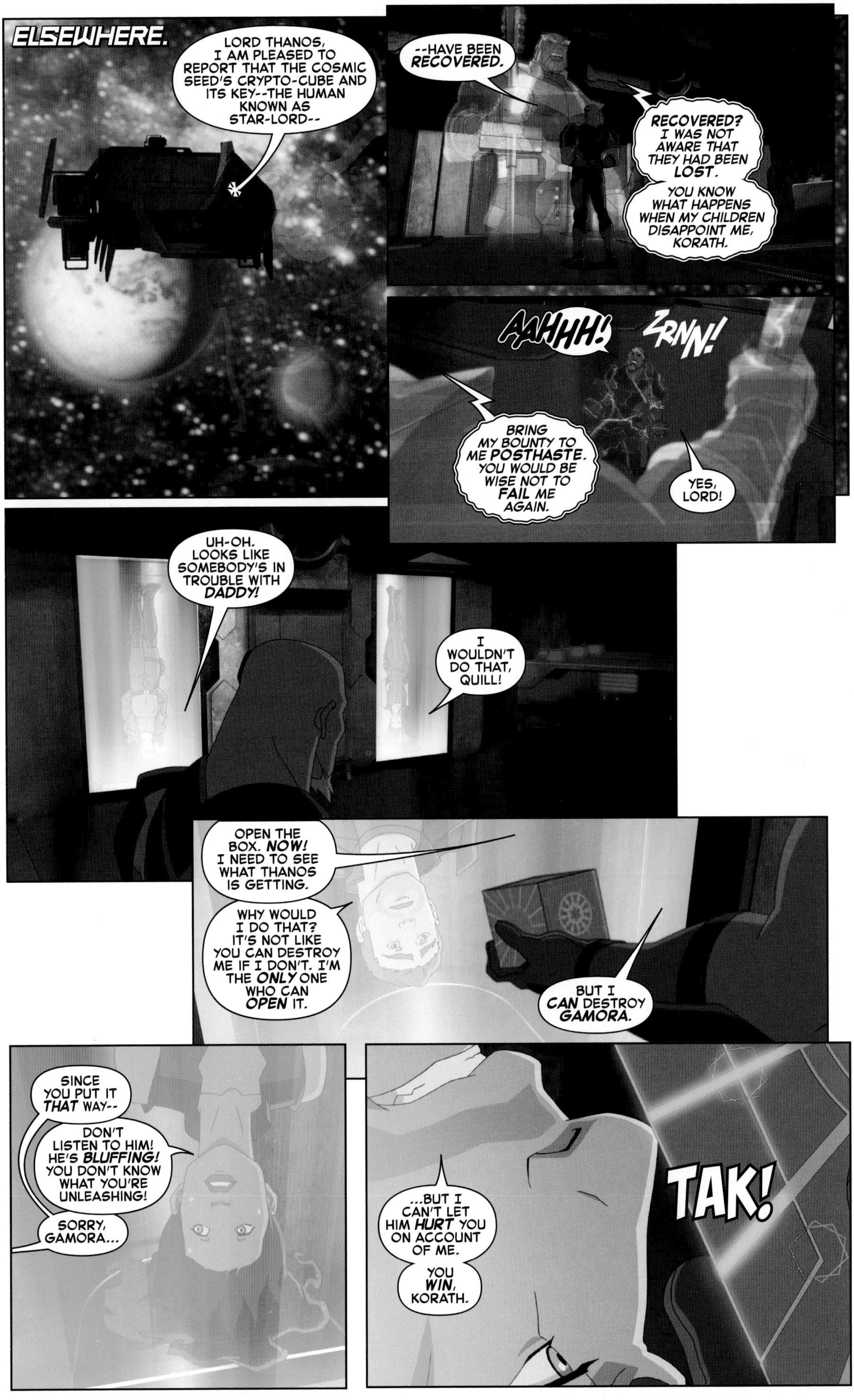
ELSEWHERE.
LORD THANOS, I AM PLEASED TO REPORT THAT THE COSMIC SEED'S CRYPTO-CUBE AND ITS KEY--THE HUMAN KNOWN AS STAR-LORD--
--HAVE BEEN RECOVERED.
RECOVERED? I WAS NOT AWARE THAT THEY HAD BEEN LOST.
YOU KNOW WHAT HAPPENS WHEN MY CHILDREN DISAPPOINT ME, KORATH.
AAHHH!
ZRNN!
BRING MY BOUNTY TO ME POSTHASTE. YOU WOULD BE WISE NOT TO FAIL ME AGAIN.
YES, LORD!
UH-OH. LOOKS LIKE SOMEBODY'S IN TROUBLE WITH DADDY!
I WOULDN'T DO THAT, QUILL!
OPEN THE BOX. NOW! I NEED TO SEE WHAT THANOS IS GETTING.
WHY WOULD I DO THAT? IT'S NOT LIKE YOU CAN DESTROY ME IF I DON'T. I'M THE ONLY ONE WHO CAN OPEN IT.
BUT I CAN DESTROY GAMORA.
SINCE YOU PUT IT THAT WAY--
DON'T LISTEN TO HIM! HE'S BLUFFING! YOU DON'T KNOW WHAT YOU'RE UNLEASHING!
SORRY, GAMORA...
...BUT I CAN'T LET HIM HURT YOU ON ACCOUNT OF ME.
YOU WIN, KORATH.
TAK!

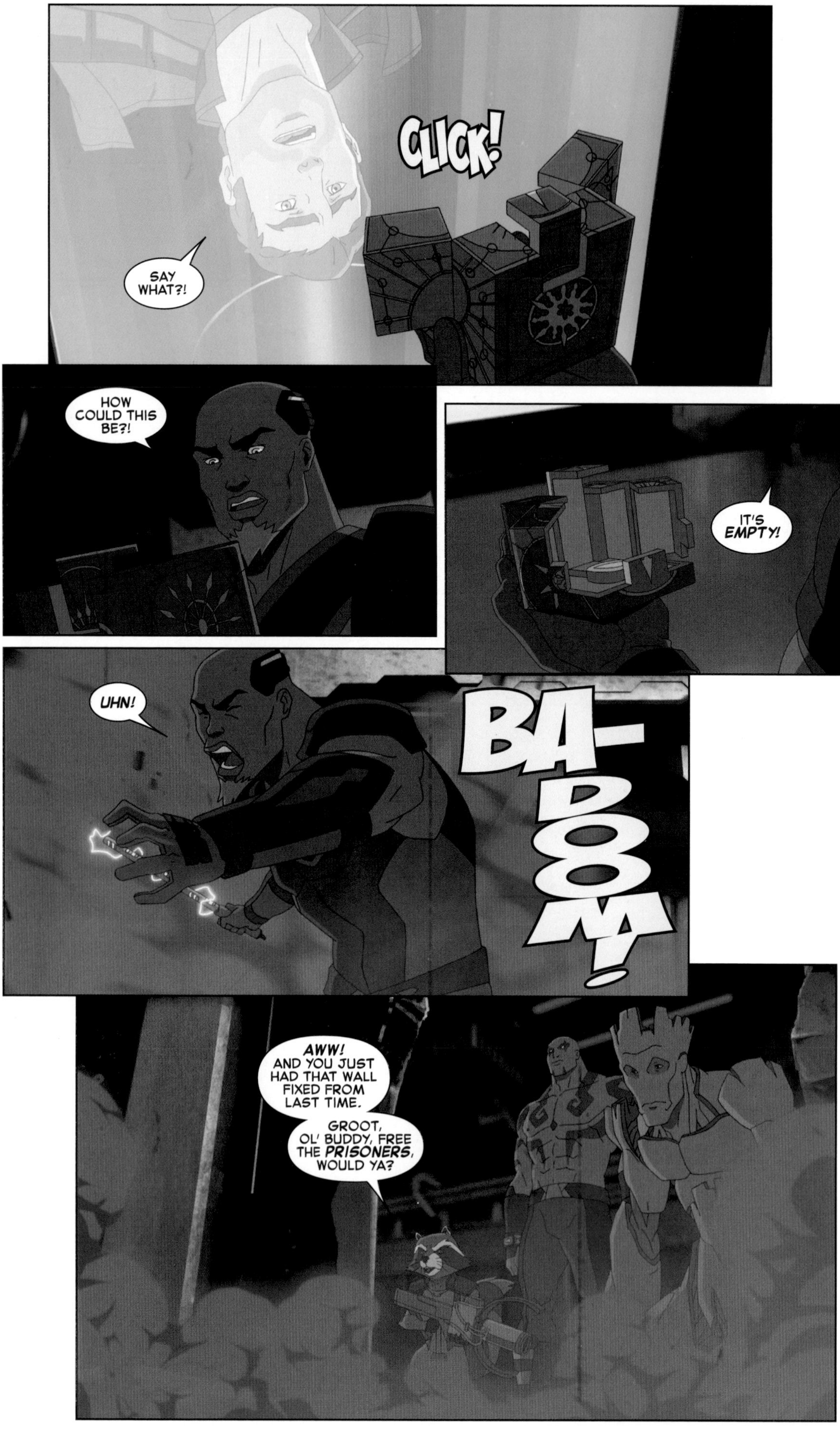
CLICK!
SAY WHAT?!
HOW COULD THIS BE?!
IT'S EMPTY!
UHN!
BA-DOOM!
AWW! AND YOU JUST HAD THAT WALL FIXED FROM LAST TIME.
GROOT, OL' BUDDY, FREE THE PRISONERS, WOULD YA?

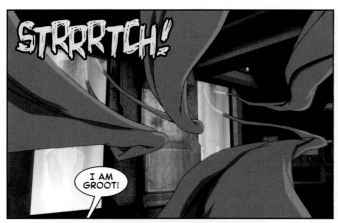

STRRRTCH!

I AM GROOT!

KRSH!

TELL THANOS THAT WHEN HE IS MAN ENOUGH TO STOP HIDING BEHIND LACKEYS AND SHOW HIS FACE...

...DRAX THE DESTROYER WILL DO TO *HIM* WHAT HE HAS DONE TO MY *FAMILY!*

OOF!

CRASH!

I DON'T KNOW HOW YOU GUYS GOT HERE SO FAST, I JUST WISH IT WAS *BEFORE* I HAD TO OPEN *THIS!*

YOU MEAN I HAD TO BUST YOUR HAIRLESS HIDE OUT OF THIS PLACE *TWICE*...

...FOR AN *EMPTY BOX?*

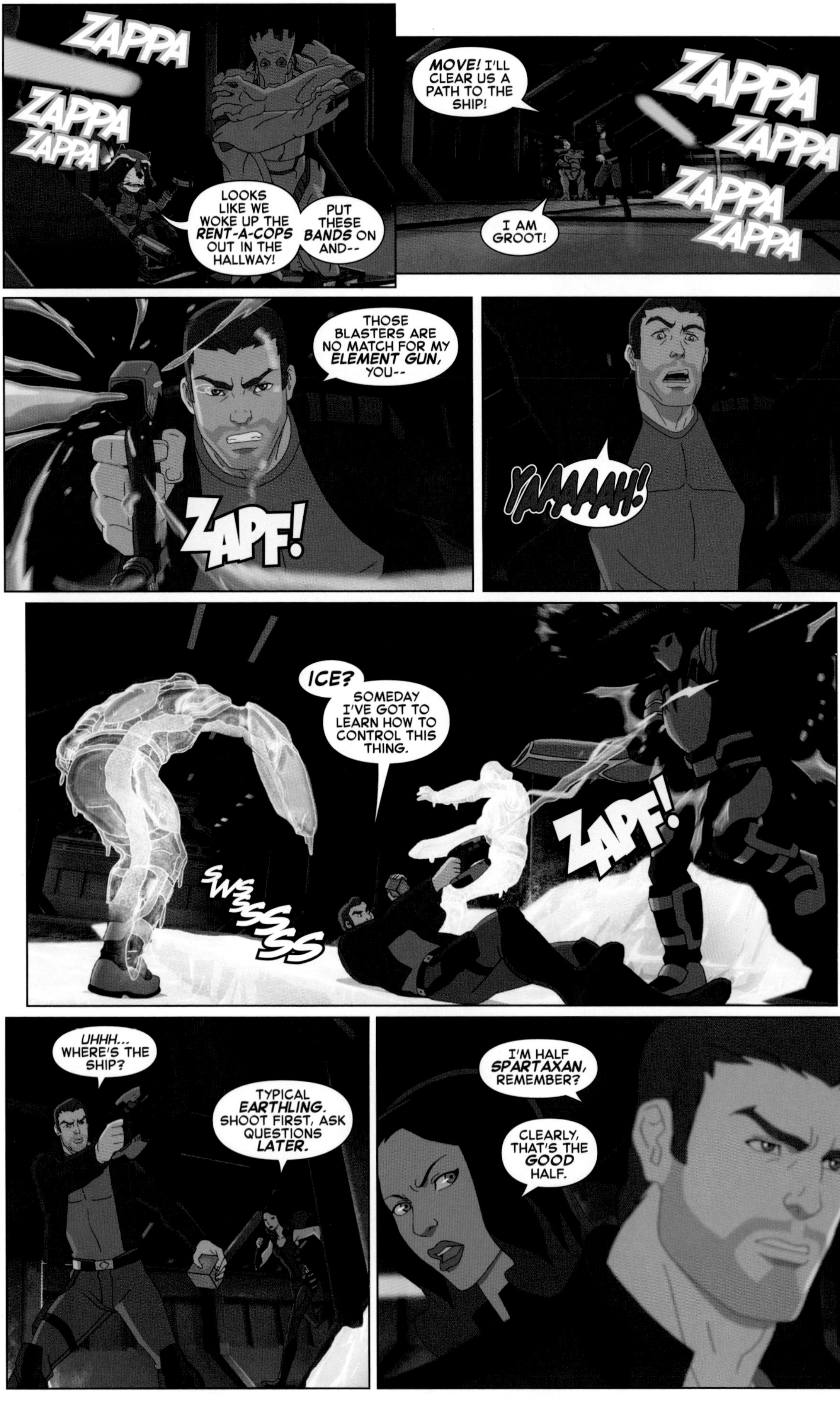
ZAPPA
ZAPPA
ZAPPA
LOOKS LIKE WE WOKE UP THE RENT-A-COPS OUT IN THE HALLWAY!
PUT THESE BANDS ON AND--
MOVE! I'LL CLEAR US A PATH TO THE SHIP!
I AM GROOT!
ZAPPA
ZAPPA
ZAPPA
ZAPPA
THOSE BLASTERS ARE NO MATCH FOR MY ELEMENT GUN, YOU--
ZAPF!
YAAAAAH!
ICE? SOMEDAY I'VE GOT TO LEARN HOW TO CONTROL THIS THING.
SWSSSSSS
ZAPF!
UHHH... WHERE'S THE SHIP?
TYPICAL EARTHLING. SHOOT FIRST, ASK QUESTIONS LATER.
I'M HALF SPARTAXAN, REMEMBER?
CLEARLY, THAT'S THE GOOD HALF.

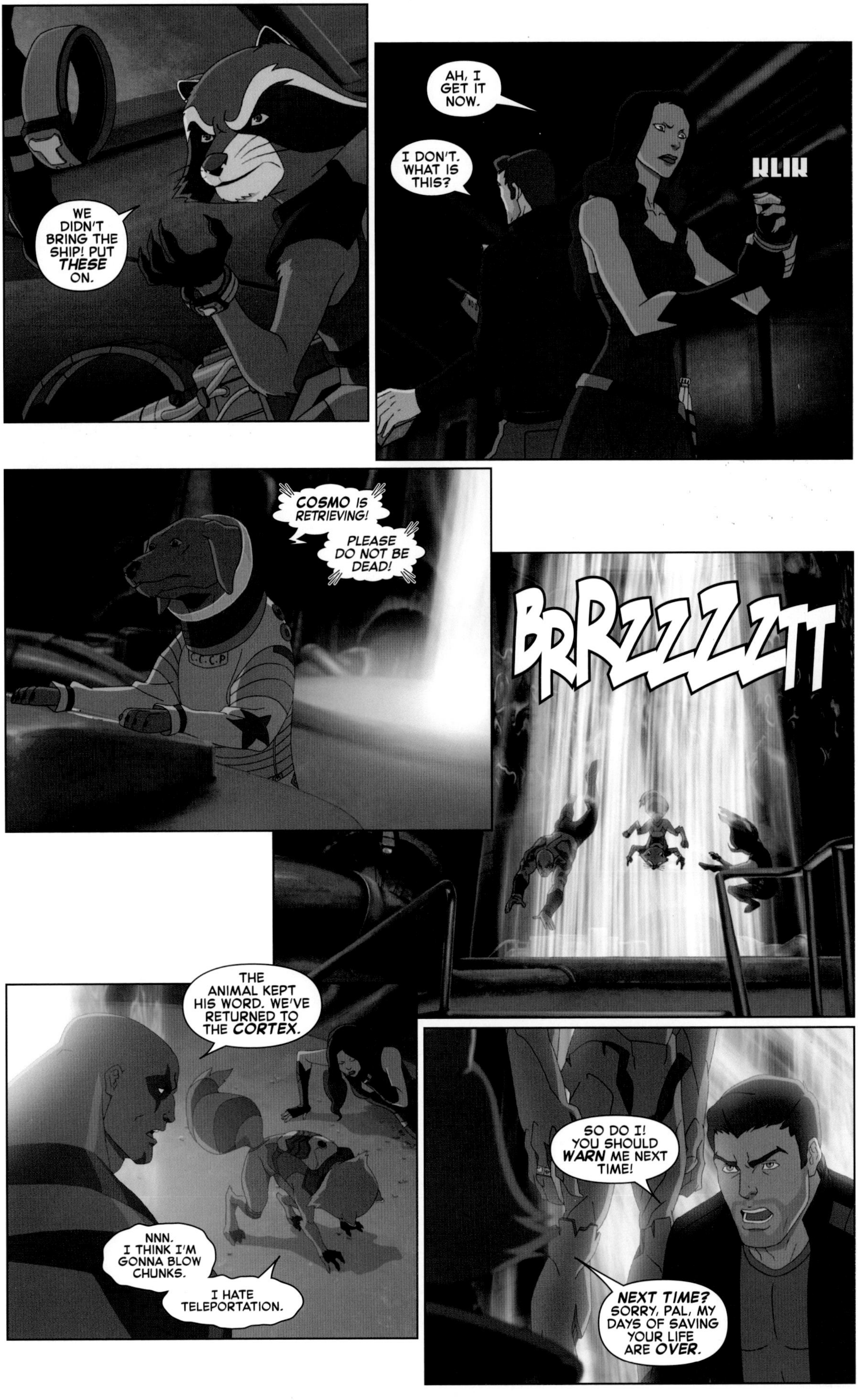
WE DIDN'T BRING THE SHIP! PUT THESE ON.
AH, I GET IT NOW.
I DON'T. WHAT IS THIS?
KLIK
COSMO IS RETRIEVING!
PLEASE DO NOT BE DEAD!
BRRZZZZZTT
THE ANIMAL KEPT HIS WORD. WE'VE RETURNED TO THE CORTEX.
NNN. I THINK I'M GONNA BLOW CHUNKS.
I HATE TELEPORTATION.
SO DO I! YOU SHOULD WARN ME NEXT TIME!
NEXT TIME? SORRY, PAL, MY DAYS OF SAVING YOUR LIFE ARE OVER.

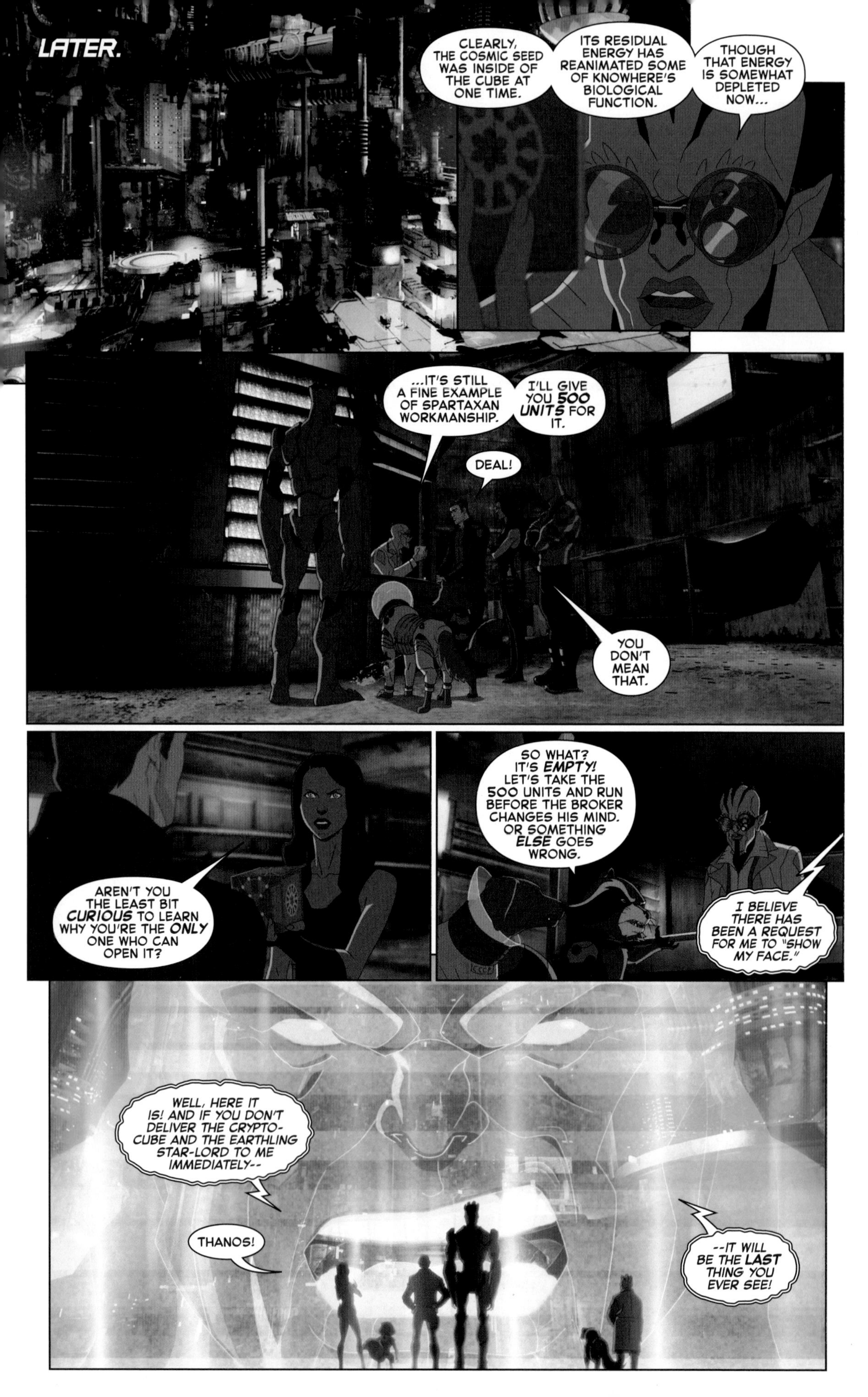
LATER.
CLEARLY, THE COSMIC SEED WAS INSIDE OF THE CUBE AT ONE TIME.
ITS RESIDUAL ENERGY HAS REANIMATED SOME OF KNOWHERE'S BIOLOGICAL FUNCTION.
THOUGH THAT ENERGY IS SOMEWHAT DEPLETED NOW...
...IT'S STILL A FINE EXAMPLE OF SPARTAXAN WORKMANSHIP.
I'LL GIVE YOU 500 UNITS FOR IT.
DEAL!
YOU DON'T MEAN THAT.
AREN'T YOU THE LEAST BIT CURIOUS TO LEARN WHY YOU'RE THE ONLY ONE WHO CAN OPEN IT?
SO WHAT? IT'S EMPTY! LET'S TAKE THE 500 UNITS AND RUN BEFORE THE BROKER CHANGES HIS MIND. OR SOMETHING ELSE GOES WRONG.
I BELIEVE THERE HAS BEEN A REQUEST FOR ME TO "SHOW MY FACE."
WELL, HERE IT IS! AND IF YOU DON'T DELIVER THE CRYPTO-CUBE AND THE EARTHLING STAR-LORD TO ME IMMEDIATELY--
THANOS!
--IT WILL BE THE LAST THING YOU EVER SEE!

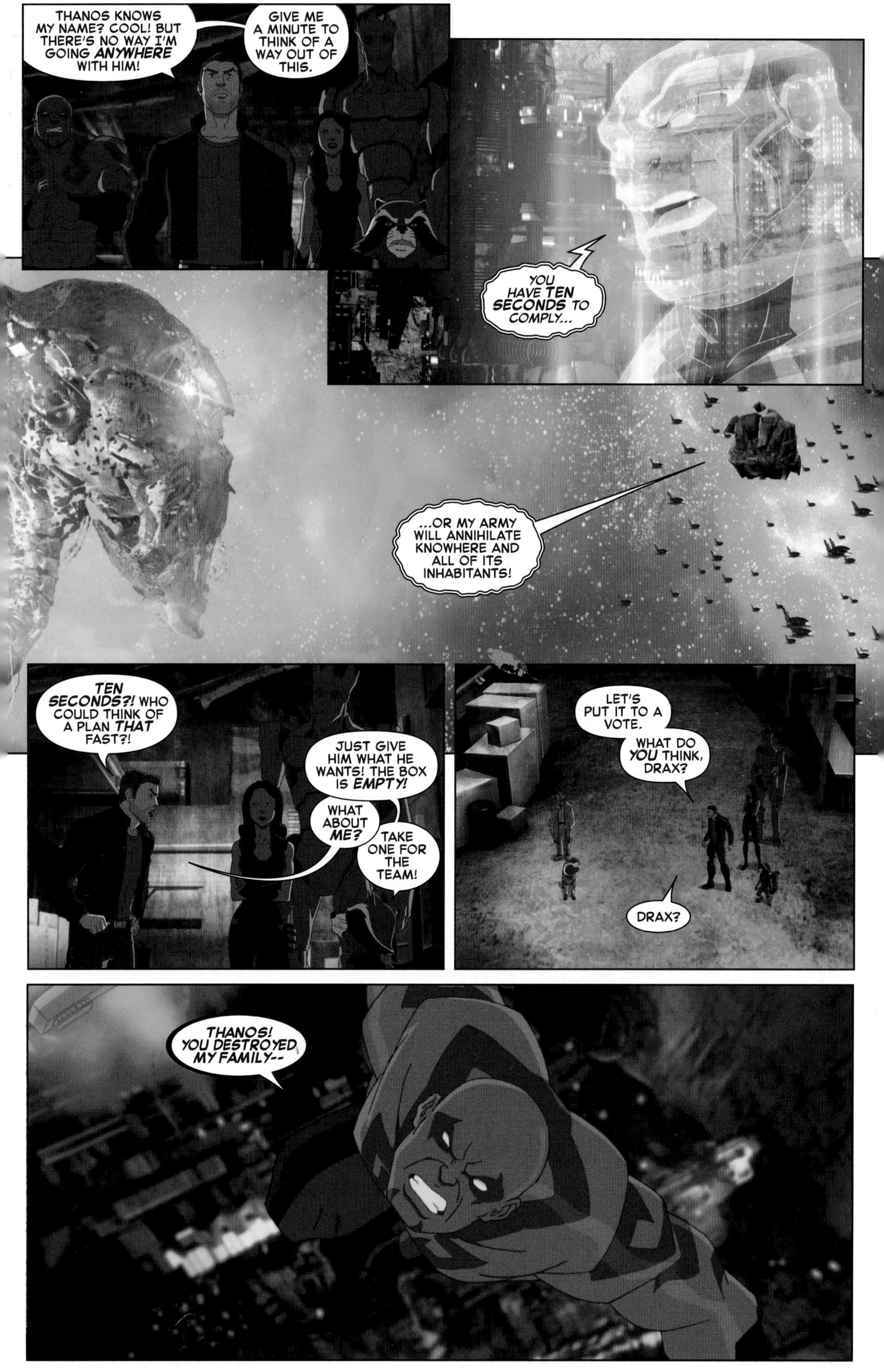
THANOS KNOWS MY NAME? COOL! BUT THERE'S NO WAY I'M GOING ANYWHERE WITH HIM!
GIVE ME A MINUTE TO THINK OF A WAY OUT OF THIS.
YOU HAVE TEN SECONDS TO COMPLY...
...OR MY ARMY WILL ANNIHILATE KNOWHERE AND ALL OF ITS INHABITANTS!
TEN SECONDS?! WHO COULD THINK OF A PLAN THAT FAST?!
JUST GIVE HIM WHAT HE WANTS! THE BOX IS EMPTY!
WHAT ABOUT ME?
TAKE ONE FOR THE TEAM!
LET'S PUT IT TO A VOTE.
WHAT DO YOU THINK, DRAX?
DRAX?
THANOS! YOU DESTROYED MY FAMILY--

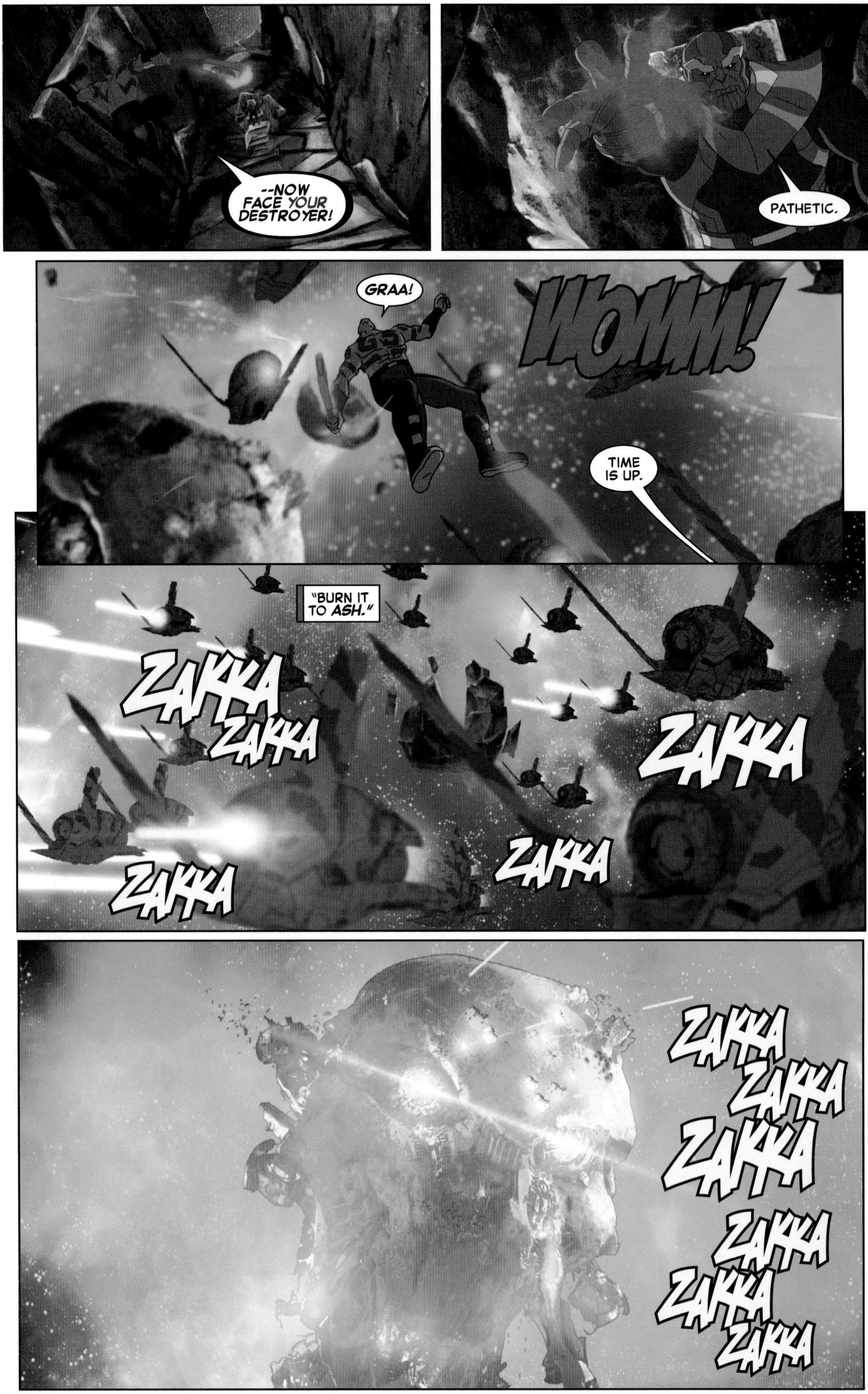
--NOW FACE YOUR DESTROYER!
PATHETIC.
GRAA!
WOMM!
TIME IS UP.
"BURN IT TO ASH."
ZAKKA ZAKKA
ZAKKA
ZAKKA
ZAKKA
ZAKKA ZAKKA ZAKKA ZAKKA ZAKKA ZAKKA

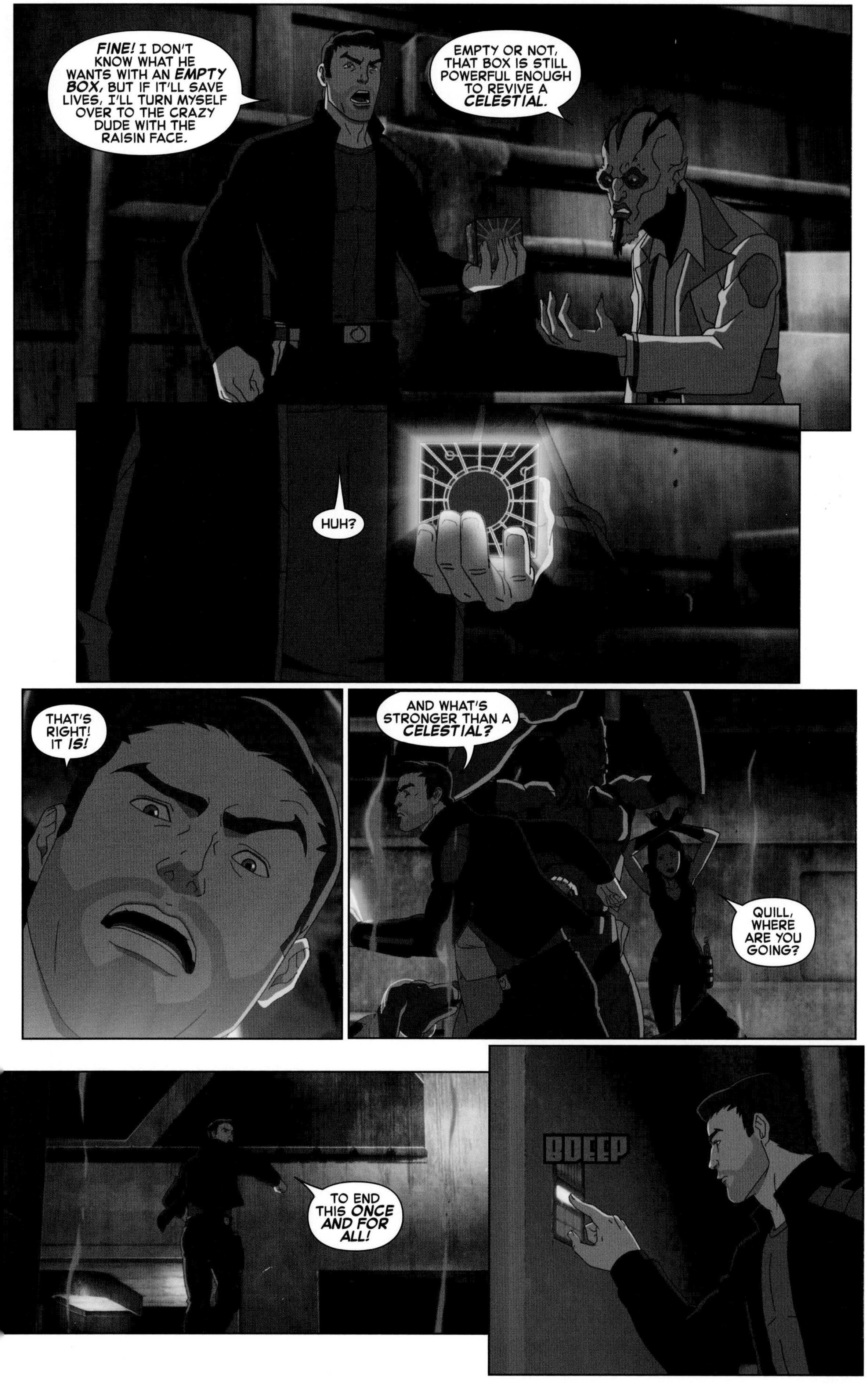
FINE! I DON'T KNOW WHAT HE WANTS WITH AN EMPTY BOX, BUT IF IT'LL SAVE LIVES, I'LL TURN MYSELF OVER TO THE CRAZY DUDE WITH THE RAISIN FACE.
EMPTY OR NOT, THAT BOX IS STILL POWERFUL ENOUGH TO REVIVE A CELESTIAL.
HUH?
THAT'S RIGHT! IT IS!
AND WHAT'S STRONGER THAN A CELESTIAL?
QUILL, WHERE ARE YOU GOING?
TO END THIS ONCE AND FOR ALL!
BDEEP

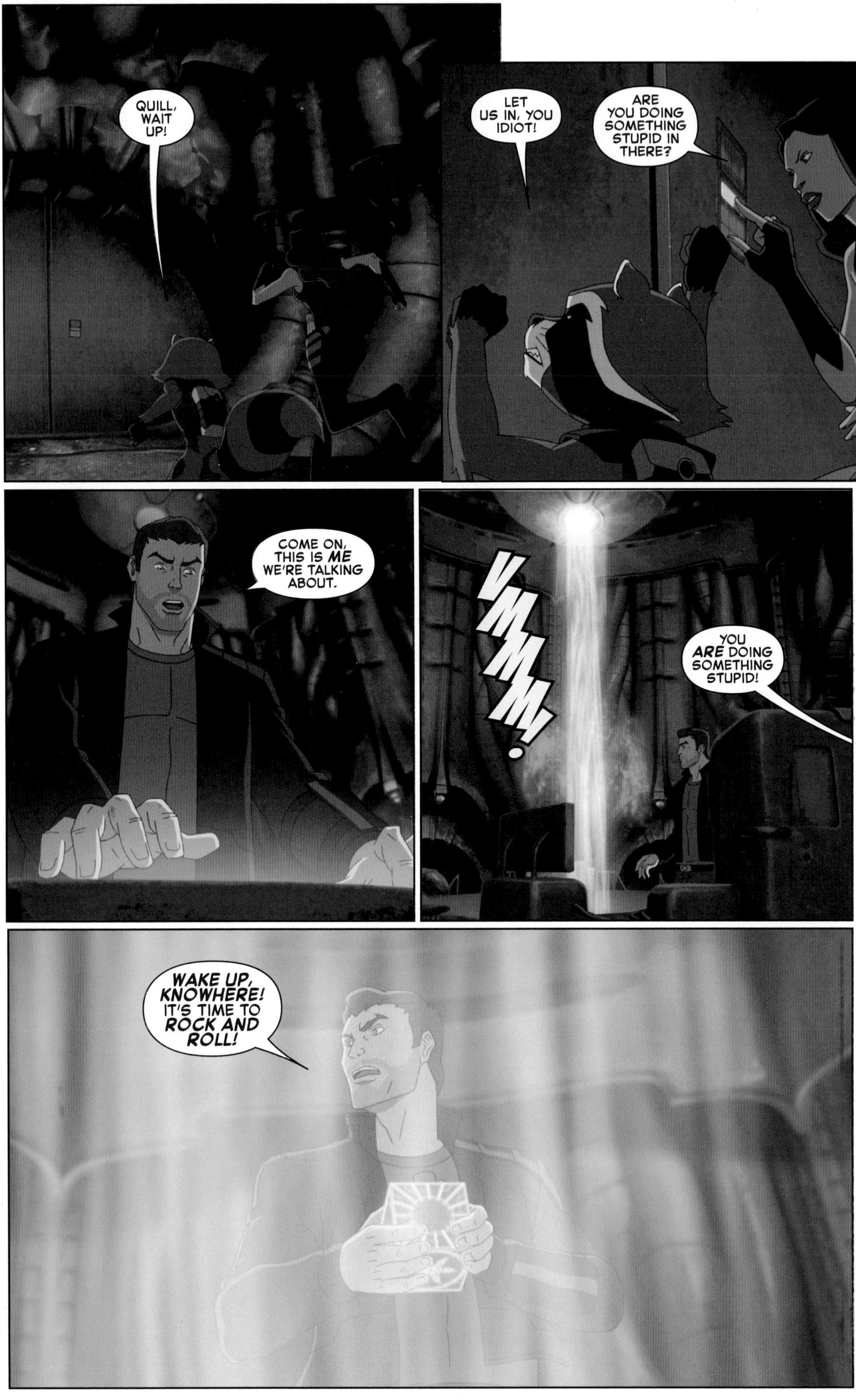
QUILL, WAIT UP!
LET US IN, YOU IDIOT!
ARE YOU DOING SOMETHING STUPID IN THERE?
COME ON, THIS IS *ME* WE'RE TALKING ABOUT.
VMMMM!
YOU *ARE* DOING SOMETHING STUPID!
WAKE UP, KNOWHERE! IT'S TIME TO *ROCK AND ROLL!*

THAT'S IT! IF YOU WON'T OPEN THE DOOR, THEN I'LL HAVE TO *BLAST* IT--

SWIK!

--OPEN?

TELEKINETIC OVERRIDE. MUCH BETTER THAN BIG BOOM, DA?

BUT NOT NEARLY AS MUCH *FUN!*

WE MUST STOP HIM BEFORE HE TELEPORTS HIMSELF INTO THE NEAREST *BLACK HOLE!*

QUILL NOT USING THE *CONTINUUM CORTEX* AS TELEPORTER--

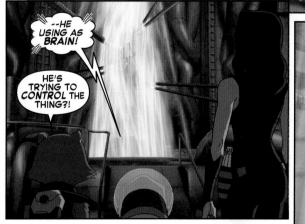

--HE USING AS *BRAIN!*

HE'S TRYING TO *CONTROL* THE THING?!

SEE? NOT SO STUPID AFTER ALL! IF THE BOX CAN BRING KNOWHERE'S *BRAIN* BACK TO LIFE, MAYBE IT CAN FIGHT BACK AGAINST THANOS'S ARMY!

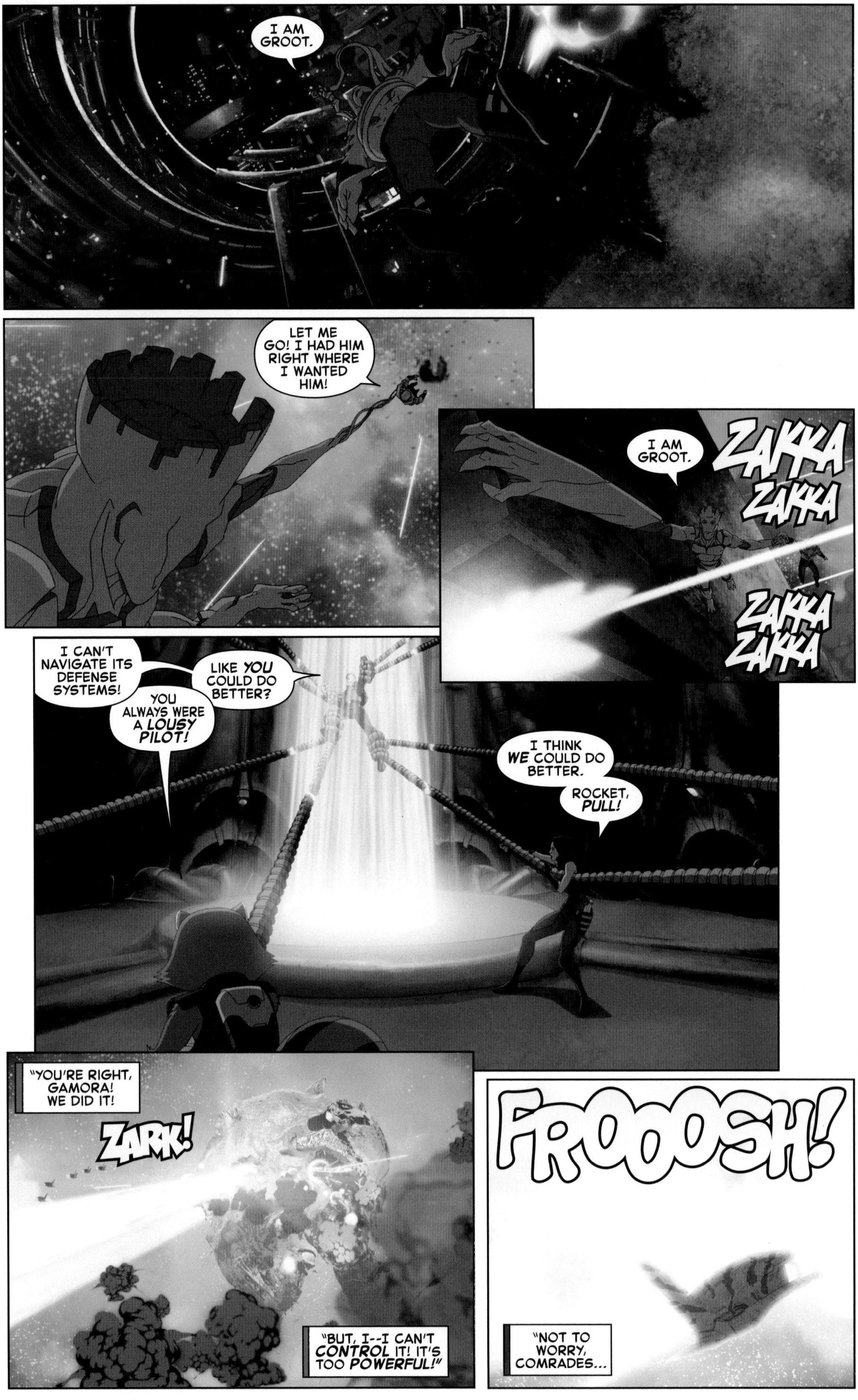
I AM GROOT.
LET ME GO! I HAD HIM RIGHT WHERE I WANTED HIM!
I AM GROOT.
ZAKKA ZAKKA
ZAKKA ZAKKA
I CAN'T NAVIGATE ITS DEFENSE SYSTEMS!
LIKE YOU COULD DO BETTER?
YOU ALWAYS WERE A LOUSY PILOT!
I THINK WE COULD DO BETTER.
ROCKET, PULL!
"YOU'RE RIGHT, GAMORA! WE DID IT!
ZARK!
"BUT, I--I CAN'T CONTROL IT! IT'S TOO POWERFUL!"
FROOOSH!
"NOT TO WORRY, COMRADES...

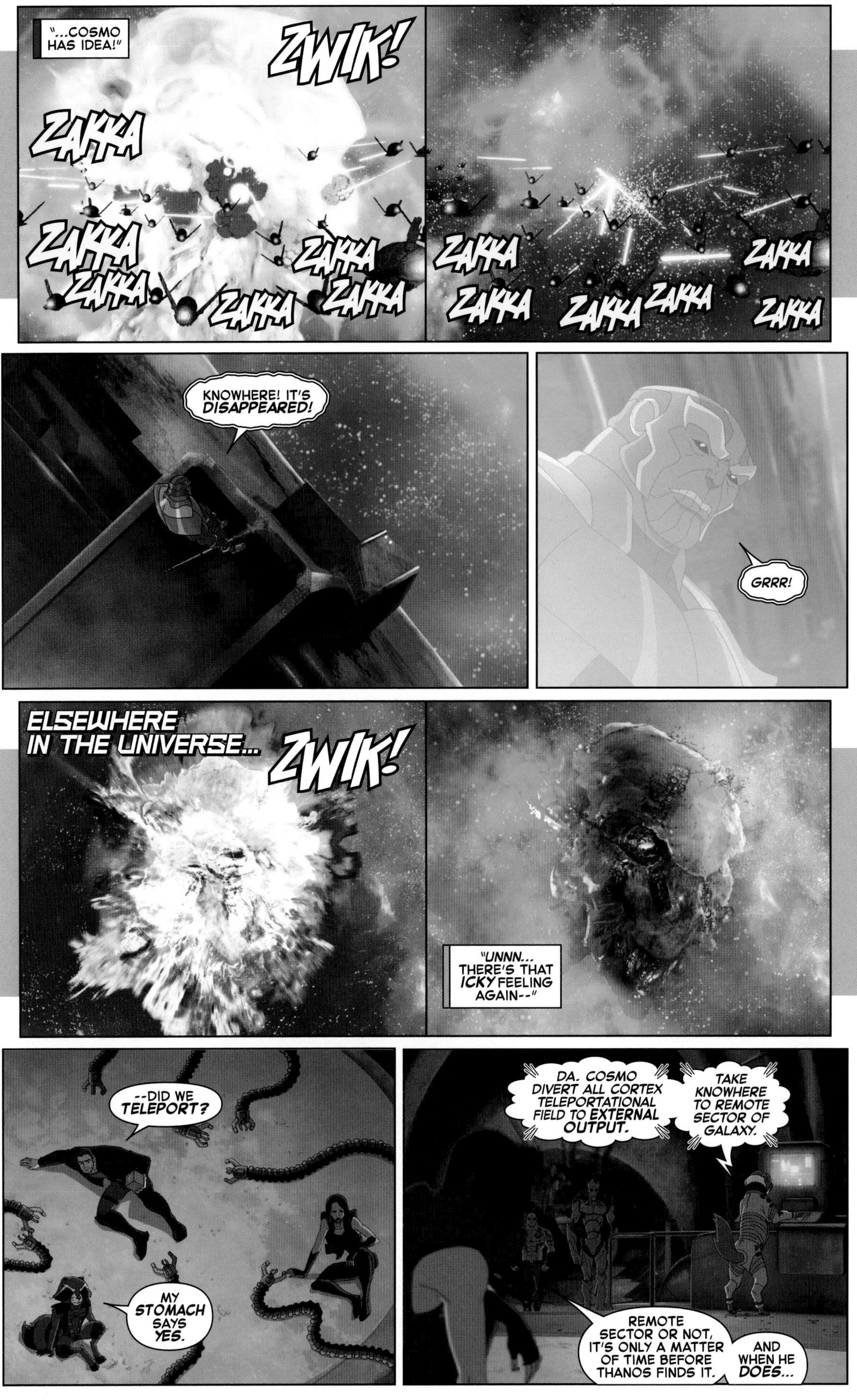
"...COSMO HAS IDEA!"
ZWIK!
ZAKKA
ZAKKA
ZAKKA
ZAKKA
ZAKKA
ZAKKA
ZAKKA
ZAKKA
ZAKKA
ZAKKA
ZAKKA
ZAKKA
KNOWHERE! IT'S DISAPPEARED!
GRRR!
ELSEWHERE IN THE UNIVERSE...
ZWIK!
"UNNN... THERE'S THAT ICKY FEELING AGAIN--"
--DID WE TELEPORT?
MY STOMACH SAYS YES.
DA. COSMO DIVERT ALL CORTEX TELEPORTATIONAL FIELD TO EXTERNAL OUTPUT.
TAKE KNOWHERE TO REMOTE SECTOR OF GALAXY.
REMOTE SECTOR OR NOT, IT'S ONLY A MATTER OF TIME BEFORE THANOS FINDS IT.
AND WHEN HE DOES...

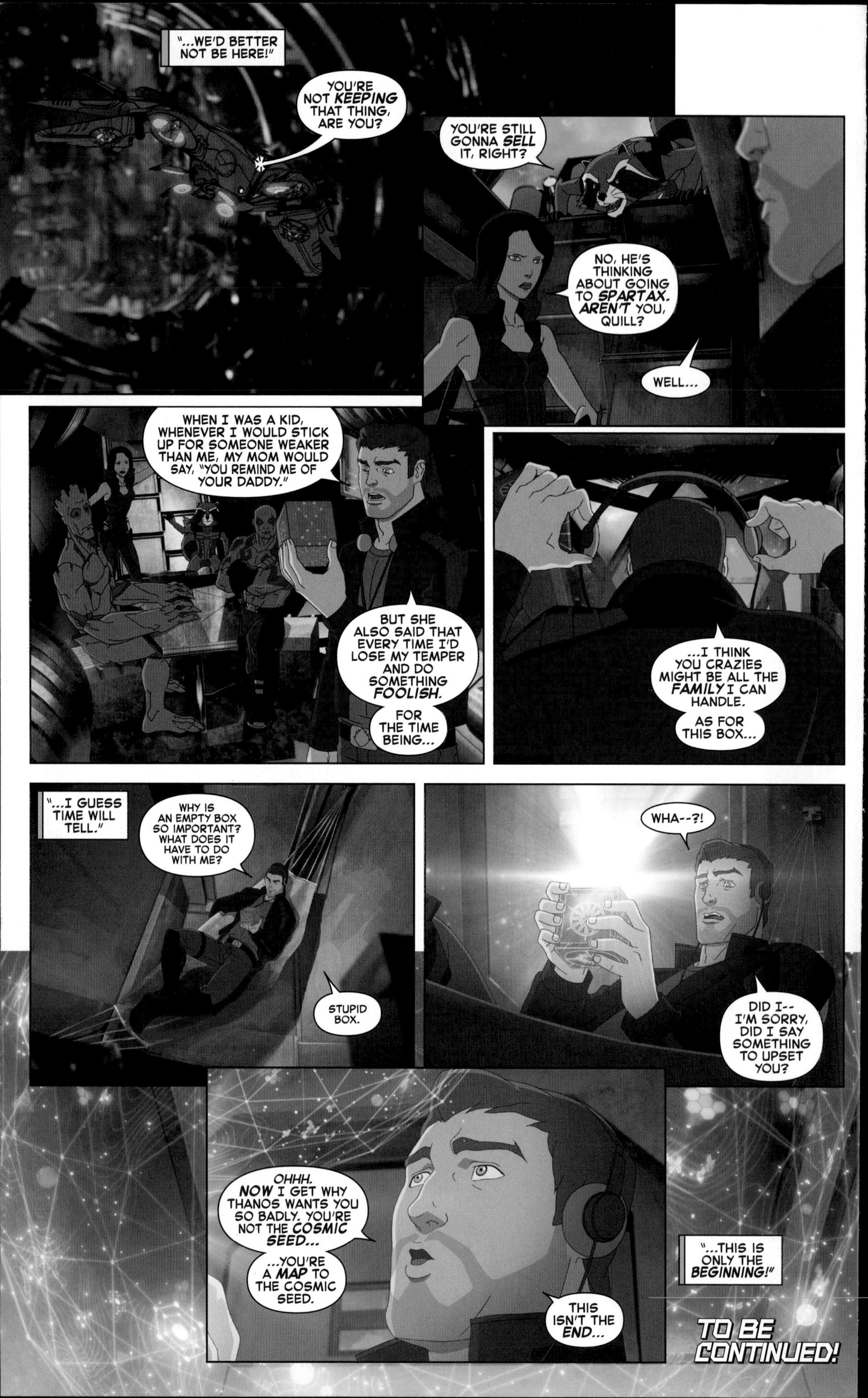
"...WE'D BETTER NOT BE HERE!"
YOU'RE NOT KEEPING THAT THING, ARE YOU?
YOU'RE STILL GONNA SELL IT, RIGHT?
NO, HE'S THINKING ABOUT GOING TO SPARTAX. AREN'T YOU, QUILL?
WELL...
WHEN I WAS A KID, WHENEVER I WOULD STICK UP FOR SOMEONE WEAKER THAN ME, MY MOM WOULD SAY, "YOU REMIND ME OF YOUR DADDY."
BUT SHE ALSO SAID THAT EVERY TIME I'D LOSE MY TEMPER AND DO SOMETHING FOOLISH.
FOR THE TIME BEING...
...I THINK YOU CRAZIES MIGHT BE ALL THE FAMILY I CAN HANDLE.
AS FOR THIS BOX...
"...I GUESS TIME WILL TELL."
WHY IS AN EMPTY BOX SO IMPORTANT? WHAT DOES IT HAVE TO DO WITH ME?
STUPID BOX.
WHA--?!
DID I-- I'M SORRY, DID I SAY SOMETHING TO UPSET YOU?
OHHH. NOW I GET WHY THANOS WANTS YOU SO BADLY. YOU'RE NOT THE COSMIC SEED...
...YOU'RE A MAP TO THE COSMIC SEED.
THIS ISN'T THE END...
"...THIS IS ONLY THE BEGINNING!"
TO BE CONTINUED!

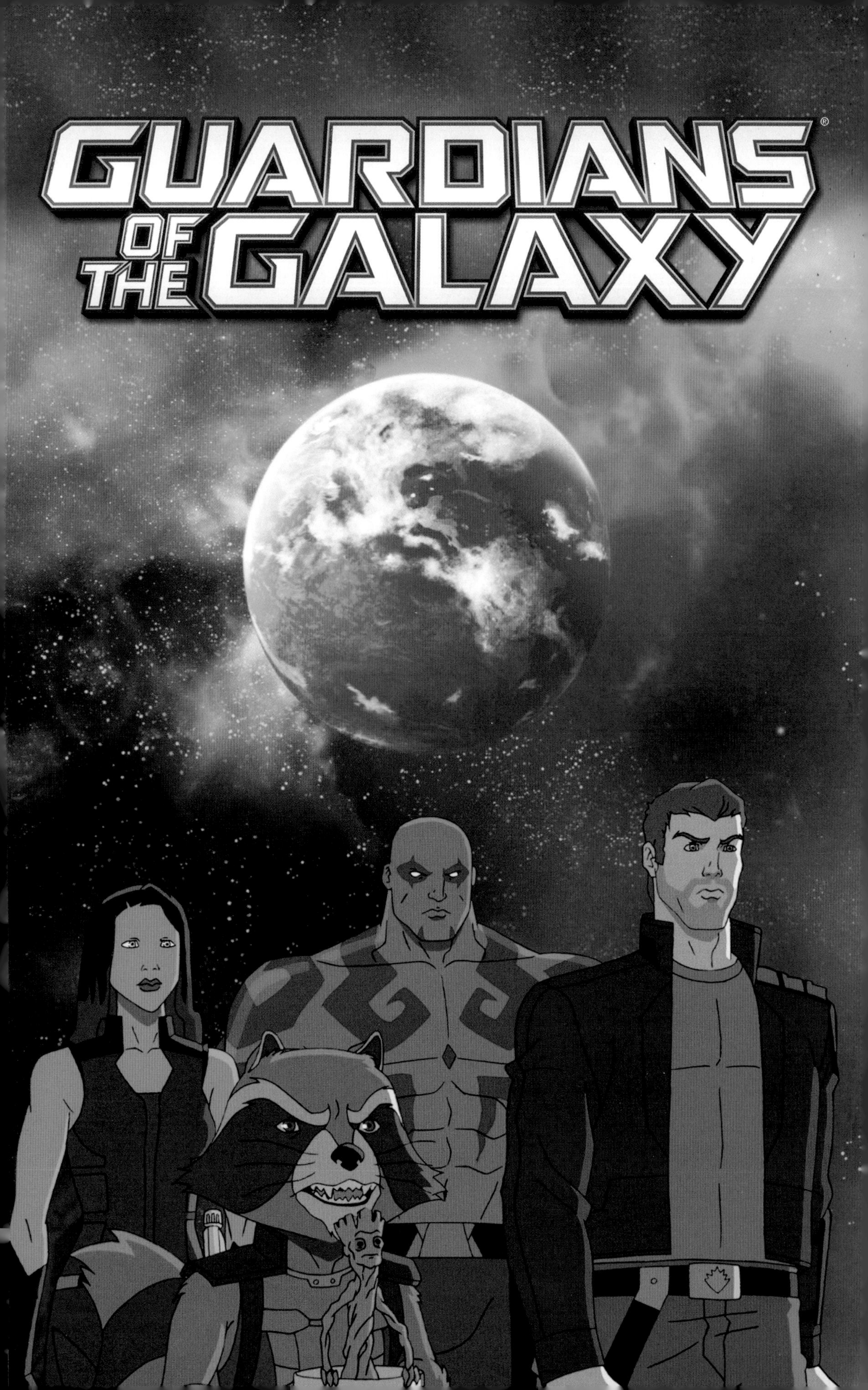
GUARDIANS OF THE GALAXY

GUARDIANS OF THE GALAXY®

COLLECT THEM ALL!

Set of 6 Hardcover Books ISBN: 978-1-5321-4069-3

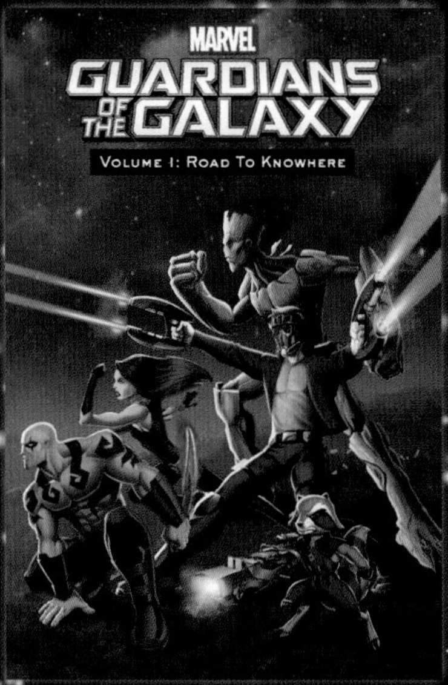
MARVEL
GUARDIANS OF THE GALAXY
Volume 1: Road To Knowhere

Hardcover Book ISBN
978-1-5321-4070-9

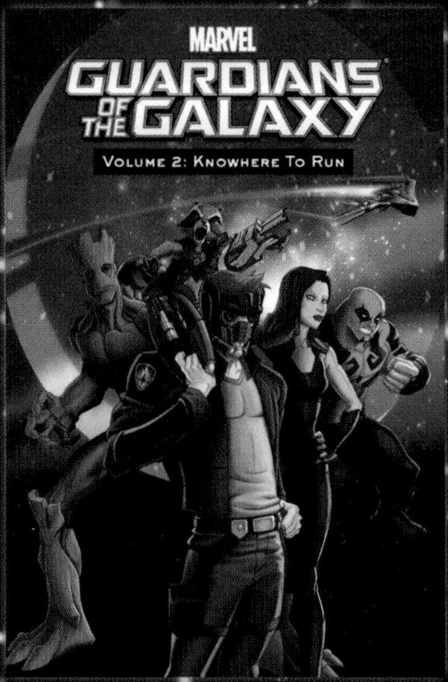
MARVEL
GUARDIANS OF THE GALAXY
Volume 2: Knowhere To Run

Hardcover Book ISBN
978-1-5321-4071-6

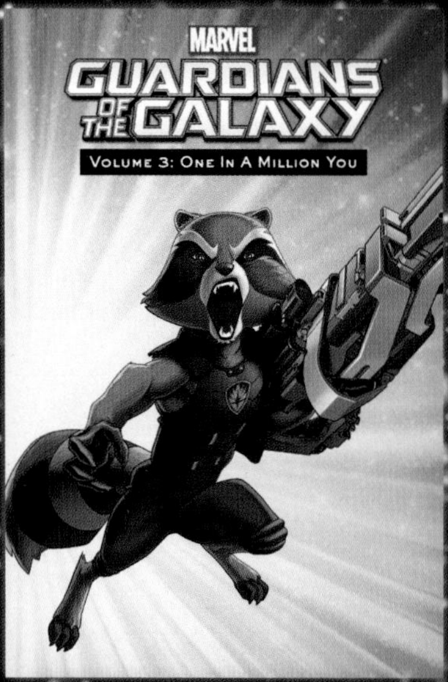
MARVEL
GUARDIANS OF THE GALAXY
Volume 3: One In A Million You

Hardcover Book ISBN
978-1-5321-4072-3

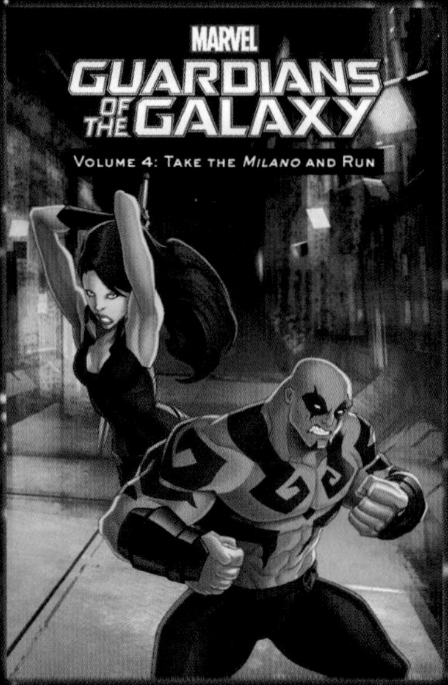
MARVEL
GUARDIANS OF THE GALAXY
Volume 4: Take the Milano and Run

Hardcover Book ISBN
978-1-5321-4073-0

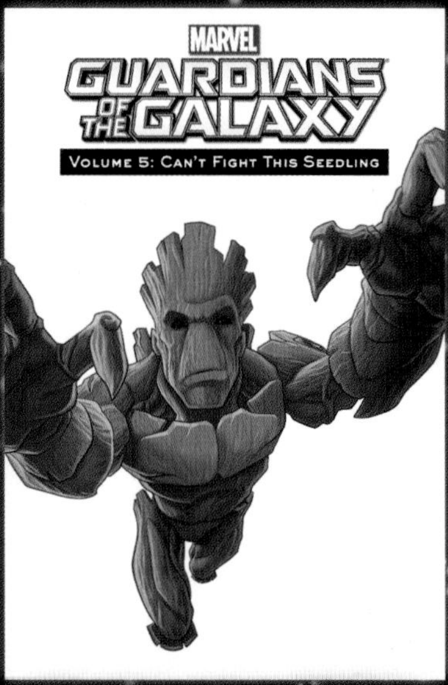
MARVEL
GUARDIANS OF THE GALAXY
Volume 5: Can't Fight This Seedling

Hardcover Book ISBN
978-1-5321-4074-7

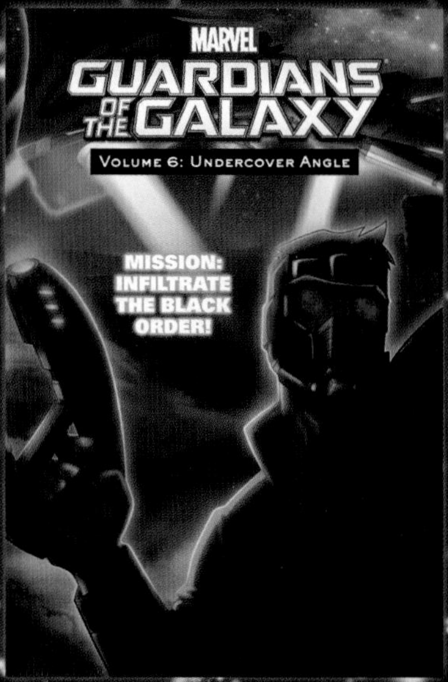
MARVEL
GUARDIANS OF THE GALAXY
Volume 6: Undercover Angle
MISSION: INFILTRATE THE BLACK ORDER!

Hardcover Book ISBN
978-1-5321-4075-4